The Treasure in the Garden

Hilary McKay

Illustrated by Tony Kenyon

VICTOR GOLLANCZ
LONDON

First published in Great Britain 1995
by Victor Gollancz
An imprint of the Cassell Group
Wellington House, 125 Strand, London WC2R 0BB

A catalogue record for this book is
available from the British Library.

ISBN 0 575 06081 6

Photoset in Great Britain by
Rowland Phototypesetting Limited,
Bury St Edmunds, Suffolk
and printed by
Guernsey Press Co. Ltd, Guernsey,
Channel Islands

To Isabel, with thanks for the garden gnome

Chapter One

Paradise House was in London. It was old and enormous and comfortable and shabby. It was a nice place to live.

For years and years there had been a rumour of something hidden at the house. Something hidden, something lost, a secret and a promise.

"Treasure perhaps!" said the hopeful children of Paradise House, but no one really knew. It was just a murmur of a story. Nobody knew where it came from, but treasure is a story one word long and nobody ever forgot it.

It was an old story. Nathan Amadi, who was nine years old, had been hearing it all his life, and the Miss Kent sisters, who lived in the opposite flat, had heard it twenty years and more earlier than that. They had been told it the day they arrived.

"But it goes back further than that," the young Miss Kent (who was only sixty) told Nathan.

"You should ask Mr McDonald," remarked the old Miss Kent.

"I asked him once," said her sister, going pink at the memory. "He was quite . . . quite . . . "

"Horrible," said Nathan understandingly, and she did not deny it. Mr McDonald, the Paradise House caretaker, was a very alarming person and Paradise House was his whole life. His parents had worked for the family who owned it when it was one big house, before it was changed into lots of small flats. They had lived in the basement. Mr McDonald's mother had helped in the kitchen and his father had driven the cars and looked after the garden. Eventually they died, and Mr McDonald took over both their jobs, living alone in the basement and getting crosser and crosser as the years went by. He did not seem to like anyone, especially children, particularly boys, and definitely not Nathan and his friend Danny.

"Look out!" said Danny as they came home from school one day. "Old McDonald is watching us!"

"Who cares about Old McDonald?" asked Nathan.

"He told my mum I stole his snails."

"*Stole his snails!*" repeated Nathan.

"Hush!" said Danny.

"Stole his snails!" said Nathan again, not hushing at all. "Why did you steal his snails?"

"I thought they'd brighten up my bedroom," explained Danny. "I didn't know he wanted them."

"What did he want them for?"

"Don't know. To eat?"

"I'm sure you can't eat snails," said Nathan.

"You can and all!" said Old McDonald unpleasantly from his doorstep.

Old McDonald's basement had windows that looked out on to a snaily wall, and to reach his front door he had to go down a flight of damp stone steps. All that Nathan and Danny could see of Old McDonald at that moment was his head, grinning a snail-eating smile at them, level with their shoes.

"On purpose?" asked Nathan, appalled but curious. "Eat snails on purpose, Mr McDonald?"

"Ho!" said Old McDonald. "All of a sudden I'm *Mr* McDonald!" and he disappeared inside and slammed the door.

"He's angry now," said Danny.

"He's always angry," said Nathan. "He's the second worst thing about Paradise House!"

The first worst thing about Paradise House was howling as Danny and Nathan pushed open the big double doors that led into the hall. Except for Old McDonald, everyone who lived there had to go through the hall before they could reach their own front doors.

"Listen to it!" said Nathan gloomily at the sound of his baby sister's shrieks. "It's been doing that for six whole weeks!"

"She smiled at me," said Danny. "She's not that bad."

"Not that bad!" repeated Nathan. "Not that bad! I'd rather live with Old McDonald!"

"He'd never have you," said Danny.

It was no secret in Paradise House that Old McDonald did not like children, but it was unlucky because the place always seemed to be full of them, racketing up and down the stairs to visit each other, or kicking their balls around the garden.

"Children!" said Old McDonald. "Yelling and fighting!" Which was not fair because the children hardly ever fought.

"Flattening the garden!" said Old McDonald, although there was really nothing to flatten, the garden of Paradise House being mostly mud and grass.

"Trailing in muck!" said Old McDonald, which was quite true; the children did trail in mud and Old McDonald was the person who had to clear it up. That was his job. To clean the stairs and hall, polish the door knocker, tidy the dustbins and to mow what was left of the grass. Old McDonald did his work very well, but very, very crossly.

"He thinks he owns Paradise House!" grumbled Nathan one day, when Old McDonald had suddenly appeared and forced him to take off his muddy trainers and pad across the hall in his socks.

"He is quite right," said Nathan's mother unsympathetically. "DON'T put those shoes down next to the baby! Or on the sofa! Or on the table! Go and find some newspaper to stand them on and scrape them clean. Look under the stairs, there's always a pile there."

Under the stairs was the big cupboard where Old McDonald kept his cleaning things, and when Nathan skidded across the hall and pulled open the door there was Old McDonald inside, sitting on the mop bucket and rubbing at a piece of old metal.

"Knock next time," said Old McDonald. "An Englishman's home is his castle and don't put them mucky things down on my clean floor!"

"I've got to clean them up," said Nathan.

Old McDonald passed him a battered knife and a newspaper.

"Scrape!" he ordered, and went back to his rubbing.

"What is it?" asked Nathan, after a few minutes of hacking at his trainers.

"Boot scraper," replied Old McDonald. "Nice bit of ironwork. I shall set it up by the steps and if you boys don't start using it, I'll have your livers!"

"What for?" asked Nathan.

"Polishing rags," said Old McDonald disagreeably.

Nathan began to cheer up. For weeks and weeks it had seemed to him that nobody had discussed anything but babies. Old McDonald's conversation was refreshingly nasty. He wondered how to bring up the subject of snails again.

"There's too many children by a long way in this house," said Old McDonald.

"Yes, there is," agreed Nathan, thinking of one he could do without.

"Baby's the only one that's no trouble," continued Old McDonald.

"No trouble!" exclaimed Nathan. "You should try living with her!"

"Ah!" said Old McDonald. "Like that, is it?"

"Awful," said Nathan.

"What's her name, then?"

"Chloe," said Nathan. "But I call her The Milk Monster."

"Charming," remarked Old McDonald. "And you call me Old McDonald! I know! You and your Mr McDonalds! I heard you!"

"Only because of the song," said Nathan hastily. "Not to be rude!"

"That right?" asked Old McDonald, glaring at him over the boot scraper.

"Well," said Nathan bravely. "To be a bit rude, too!"

"Good!" said Old McDonald, grinning like a letter-box. "Tell the truth and shame the devil! I can see you wasn't put together with spit! And what do they call you?"

"Nathan," said Nathan, completely overwhelmed by Old McDonald's horrible compliments.

"I don't like fancy-pants names," remarked Old McDonald.

"It isn't!" said Nathan indignantly.

"Never said it was," said Old McDonald. "What's that boy who lives at the top called, then?"

"Danny."

"What about the girl underneath?"

"Anna."

"All the same when it comes to trailing in muck," said Old McDonald. "And I don't know what you're laughing at! Get on with them boots!"

"I am getting on," said Nathan, carefully digging wedges of dried mud from the soles of his trainers.

"You're spinning it out. You'll be here all night."

"I shouldn't mind. It's nice in here."

"Nice?"

"Peaceful," explained Nathan, grinning suddenly at Old McDonald.

This boy is not afraid of me, thought Old McDonald. He ought to be, but he isn't! He's enjoying himself scraping boots in the cupboard under the stairs. With me! And I've not been soft with him, either. I've told him what I think.

"Look at this scraper!" said Old McDonald out loud. "It's come up lovely! I'll have it kept like that, don't you forget. You lot clean it off when you've used it!"

"Clean the boot scraper?" asked Nathan, astonished.

"Or I'll have your livers," said Old McDonald.

"What are we supposed to clean it with?"

"I shall find an old brush."

"It'll get lost in no time."

"I shall tie it on with string," said Old McDonald. "Them boots of yours is clean."

Nathan sighed.

"Give them a spit and polish," said Old McDonald, passing Nathan a piece of old vest. "What did you say your name was?"

"Nathan," said Nathan, spitting on his trainers.

"Good name," said Old McDonald.

"So is Old McDonald," said Nathan. "I shall be a farmer when I grow up."

"They've called me Old McDonald since I was a boy," Old McDonald told him.

"Do you mind?"

"Sticks and stones may break my bones," said Old McDonald, "but calling never hurt me."

"That's not true, though," said Nathan.

"No, it ain't," agreed Old McDonald. "What did you tell me you called that baby?"

"I shall call her Chloe," said Nathan. "But I wish she'd shut up screaming."

"You come in here when you want a bit of peace," said Old McDonald.

"In here?"

"You could tell your mum. She'd know

where you were. You could bring a book."

"Wouldn't you mind?"

"I shouldn't have to," said Old McDonald.

"Thank you," said Nathan.

"You make a mess and I'll string you up," warned Old McDonald.

"I never shall," promised Nathan.

"I used to have a farm once," Old McDonald told him.

"A real farm?"

"Real enough to me."

"When?" asked Nathan.

"When I was about your age," said Old McDonald. "There's your mum calling."

"What happened to the farm?" asked Nathan.

"I was robbed," said Old McDonald.

"Old McDonald is the nicest person I know," Nathan told Danny as they walked to school the next morning.

"You must know some awful people, then," said Danny.

"He said I can sit in his place under the stairs."

"He can't make you do it. Tell your mum."

"He offered. Whenever I like."

"Whenever *you* like?"

"For a sort of den."

There was a lot of difference, to Danny's mind, between sitting under the stairs because Old McDonald made you, and sitting under the stairs of your own free will.

"Just you?" asked Danny hopefully.

"I might let you come sometimes," said Nathan kindly.

"After school?"

"Not straight after school. I've got to help Old McDonald put up a boot scraper."

"Can't he put up a boot scraper on his own?"

"He said he'd wait for me," said Nathan calmly, as if putting up boot scrapers with Old McDonald was a perfectly natural thing to do. "I might be in there later, though."

"How shall I know?"

"Knock," said Nathan.

Chapter Two

The following morning was a Saturday. Nathan disappeared at first light so as to waste no time moving into his new home.

"Don't forget about Danny!" his mother called after him.

"What about Danny?" asked Nathan, pausing for a moment.

"His mother's working today, so he's stopping for lunch with us."

"Well, he knows where I'll be," replied Nathan, sounding much more cheerful than he had for a long time.

Which is all thanks to Old McDonald, thought his mother. Six weeks of sulking had been hard to bear and she was so pleased it was over that she baked a batch of scones for Old McDonald, collected Chloe, and took them down to the basement.

"I like 'em a bit burnt," said Old McDonald, inspecting his present with care. "Nothing like a bit of burnt baking for helping the wind!"

"What wind?" asked Nathan's mother, glancing up and resisting the impulse to grab back her beautiful golden scones and hit him with the tray.

"Belly wind," explained Old McDonald. "A bit of burnt shifts it beautiful!"

"Goodness!" said Nathan's mother, staring at him in horror.

"Well-known fact," said Old McDonald complacently. "Now then, young Chloe! You're the only person in the house who doesn't trail in muck!"

"He has a heart of gold," Nathan's mother told herself as she climbed back up the steps. "Gold!" Old McDonald had dug into his pockets and produced a pound coin that he pressed into Chloe's fat hand. "For luck!" he explained, and had recommended rum to stop the screaming.

"All right, Nathan?" called his mother as she passed the cupboard under the stairs.

24

"Perfect," said Nathan, appearing at the door.

"Perfect!" she exclaimed when she saw him. "What have you been doing? Look at you! You are filthy!"

"Only in patches," said Nathan cheerfully.

"Very large patches!" replied his mother crossly. "And your jumper and jeans were clean on this morning. And what do you think you're doing with your quilt in there?"

"I've been making a place to sleep."

"Oh no, you don't!" said his mother.

"Please," begged Nathan. "Just until Chloe grows up."

"Definitely not!"

"There's stacks of space, much more than in my bedroom. Come and look."

To please him, his mother stepped inside and looked around. As far as she could see it looked exactly as it always had, a large, dimly lit cupboard with a ceiling that sloped from the doorway right down to the floor, and an enormous amount of junk stored at the back. But to Nathan the cupboard meant freedom. He had heaped the boxes of junk to one side to make room for a bed and had constructed himself a sofa out of piles of newspaper.

"Sit down," he said to his mother, patting the newspaper sofa, "and I'll shut the door and you can see how quiet it is."

Obediently his mother sat down.

"It is quiet," she admitted after a few moments. "And private. I can see why you like it."

"Anna likes it, too," said Nathan. "Except for the spiders."

"What spiders?" asked his mother.

"They kept running out of the newspaper when I was making the sofa," explained Nathan.

"Oh," said his mother. "I think I shall have to go."

"Can I sleep here, then?"

"Nope!"

"Well, can me and Danny have our lunch in here?"

"I suppose so," agreed his mother. "If you wash your hands first, and if you don't mind sandwiches, and if Danny doesn't object. Where is Danny? I haven't seen him all morning."

"He's outside digging for badgers," Nathan told her.

"Digging for badgers?"

"I'm sure that's what he said. I'll go and tell him about lunch."

Danny, when Nathan asked him, said he would love to have lunch in the cupboard under the stairs, and he abandoned his spade and hurried indoors.

"You need a bath!" said Nathan's mother when she saw him.

"It's clean dirt," said Danny vaguely.

"Did you find any?"

"What?"

"Nathan said you were digging for badgers."

"Digging *holes* for badgers," explained Danny. "Holes for them to live in," he added, seeing the bewildered expression on her face.

"Like blue tit boxes," he told her, but she only looked more confused than ever.

*　　*　　*

It was Danny who noticed the picture.

Lunch was over. Nathan flopped back on his quilt and pretended to go to sleep, but when Danny tried to flop on the sofa it collapsed into a heap of newspapers and deposited him on to the floor.

"Don't mess up my house," murmured Nathan.

"I didn't mean to. Anyway, it's really Old McDonald's house."

"He doesn't live here."

"He must have done once, or someone must have, if it wasn't Old McDonald. They put up a picture."

"A picture?" Nathan sat up. "Where? I never noticed a picture."

"Over there, pinned on to the wall." Danny pointed to the darkest corner of the cupboard. "I can only see half of it because of the light but it's a proper painted picture. It's a house."

"Perhaps it's a picture of Paradise House," suggested Nathan, crawling over Danny and the newspapers to inspect it. "No, it can't be, there's no front door and

the garden's too big."

"It's not very good," said Danny. "It looks home-made, and it's very old! Look at the drawing pins, they've all gone rusty."

"It reminds me of something," said Nathan, staring at the picture with a puzzled face. "The house has a window just like the one in your bedroom. Look! Even the bars are painted on. And there's the drainpipe that broke when Anna climbed it. It *is* Paradise House! It's Paradise House from the back! Let's get it off the wall and look at it properly!"

The picture had been painted on thick white card and looked as if it had been stuck on the wall for years and years. The drawing pins that held it were crumbling with rust and there was a square patch of mildew on the plaster behind, where dampness had collected.

"It's all mouldy," said Danny, disappointed.

"Only a bit," said Nathan, carrying it into the light. "And, look, it's got writing on the back!"

The back of the cardboard was stained with mildew, but not so stained that the words written there could not be read.

"It doesn't look very important," said Danny, glancing again at the picture. "It looks very boring. Just a house and a garden and lots of flowers. Roses. I don't believe Paradise House ever had that many roses!"

"There's somebody digging the roses. It looks like a boy," said Nathan, peering at the picture more closely. "And there's somebody in your window pointing down at the person digging. Let's go and show it to Old McDonald."

"You wouldn't dare!" said Danny.

"Of course I would!"

"Oh," said Danny.

"I bet you're too scared to come with me!"

"I bet I'm not!" said Danny but there was a quiver in his voice that Nathan noticed.

"Old McDonald is a nice old man," he told Danny encouragingly. "He gave Chloe a pound and my mum says he has a heart of gold."

"You should have heard him going on about those snails," said Danny.

"I'm not put together with spit!" remarked Nathan meaningfully.

"Oh, all right," said Danny.

Chapter Three

Old McDonald stood at the bottom of the basement steps, rubbing his stomach and groaning.

"Hallo," said Danny to prove to Nathan that he was not scared.

"I hope you've not come for no more of my snails," said Old McDonald, still rubbing his stomach.

"You can't have eaten all of them," said Danny, staring at Old McDonald's stomach in disbelief. "There were hundreds!"

"Boy's a fool," said Old McDonald, to no one in particular, and groaned again.

"Are you ill?" asked Nathan.

"I got a terrible bloat," said Old McDonald.

"A terrible what?"

"Them buns of your mum's. But say

nothing to her. She meant no harm."

"My mum's a brilliant cook," said Nathan, bristling.

"Well, she slipped up on them buns," replied Old McDonald. "And I should know because I ate 'em."

"All of them?"

"There was nowt but a mouthful."

"There was *twelve*!" said Nathan. "You deserve a terrible bloat!"

"I do, do I?" asked Old McDonald.

"Especially on top of snails!"

"I shall never hear the last of them snails," remarked Old McDonald. "What's that you're holding?"

"It's a picture we found under the stairs."

"You didn't find it because it wasn't lost," said Old McDonald.

"Did you know it was there, then?" asked Danny.

"Of course I knew."

"Is it Paradise House?"

"What does it look like?"

"Do you know who painted it?"

"What do you take me for?"

"Who are the people? The person in the room with bars and the person digging in the garden?"

"Who do you think?"

"Why was it painted and stuck up on the wall?"

"How should I know?"

"Did Paradise House really have a garden like that? All those roses?"

"Why else would they call it Paradise House?" asked Old McDonald.

"He didn't tell us much," said Danny, when they were safely back home and under the stairs again.

"No," agreed Nathan absent-mindedly, still examining the picture. "But he told us it was Paradise House, didn't he? And why it's called Paradise House. I've always wondered. And he told us he knew the person who painted it."

"Did he?" asked Danny, surprised.

"And he told us we knew the people in the picture. Or ought to know. I'm sure the one digging is Old McDonald!"

"It can't be!"

"It is," said Nathan, perfectly certain. "You look. Same gingery hair . . . "

"Old McDonald's hair is grey."

"Grey and ginger mixed," said Nathan. "Same sort of hunchy way of standing. Same sort of shape. Same sort of baggy blue trousers . . . "

"The person in the picture is a boy!" interrupted Danny.

"So was Old McDonald when the picture was painted," pointed out Nathan triumphantly. "And I bet when Old McDonald was a boy he looked just like that! Anyway, who else do we know that it might have been?"

At last Danny was beginning to understand Nathan's reasoning.

"I bet the person who painted the picture is the person in the window!" he announced.

"Peter Jonathan Hunter," said Nathan.

"Because Old McDonald and Peter Jonathan Hunter are the only people we know that it could possibly be."

"That's right," said Nathan.

"Because we don't know anyone else from then."

"Yes," said Nathan. "Peter Jonathan Hunter painted the picture and stuck it up on the wall under the stairs when he and Old McDonald were boys."

"Perhaps Peter Jonathan Hunter's bedroom was my bedroom," said Danny. "It used to be the nursery when Paradise House was a posh house. Perhaps Peter and Old McDonald used to play together. Perhaps they made under the stairs into their den, and that's why Old McDonald thought you would like it."

"He didn't really talk as if they were friends, though," said Nathan. "Perhaps they quarrelled."

"Why did Peter paint the picture and stick it on the wall?" wondered Danny.

"Old McDonald didn't tell us that," said Nathan. "He didn't know."

They gazed at the picture in silence.

"Perhaps it doesn't matter," said Danny eventually. "Perhaps it's just a picture stuck on a wall."

"Peter thought it mattered," said Nathan. "He thought it was very important."

There were voices in the hall outside; Nathan's mother was talking to the two Miss Kents from the other ground-floor flat.

"Poor Nathan has moved into the cupboard under the stairs," Nathan heard his mother telling them, and they clucked sympathetically.

"Hallo!" he said, popping his head out of the door.

"Hallo!" said his mother. "Is Danny with you? His mother is waiting for him. She wants to get to the shops before they shut. We checked a few minutes ago but you'd disappeared."

"We went to see Old McDonald," explained Nathan, while Danny reluctantly took himself upstairs. "We found out why Paradise House is called Paradise House. Because of all the roses that used to grow in the garden."

"Did he tell you that?" asked one of the old ladies. "Well, he should know if anyone

does. He's lived here since before the war."

"What war?" asked Nathan.

"Nathan!" exclaimed his mother. "Don't they teach you anything at school?"

"The Second World War," the oldest Miss Kent told him kindly. "That was a very long time ago now, I suppose. I was just about your age when it began."

"How awful for you," remarked Nathan's mother.

"Not really," replied Miss Kent. "Quite an adventure in a way. We children were tremendously excited at the thought of air raids, and then, the next summer, in nineteen-forty, we were all sent off to the country. I thought I'd gone to heaven!"

"In nineteen-forty?" asked Nathan, becoming suddenly alert. "Did everyone go?" And the old ladies, very pleased at his interest, explained how nearly every child in London had been packed off to the country to escape the bombing.

"Train-loads of children," they told him. "Each with nothing but one small case and a gasmask in a box!"

"What about all their toys?" asked Nathan.

"Toys were left behind," they told him.

"I squeezed in my paintbox," remembered the young Miss Kent, "and a book I couldn't bear to part with. We left behind a beautiful doll's house that we never saw again."

"What a pity!" exclaimed Nathan's mother but the Miss Kents shook their heads and said, no, no, no, somebody would have enjoyed it.

"We were tomboys, really," said the old Miss Kent.

That evening Nathan found four drawing pins and fastened the picture back on to the wall where he and Danny had found it. Then, for a long time, he sat and wondered. Old McDonald came up to look for something and was startled to find him still sitting there.

"You been here all day?" he asked, quite gently for Old McDonald.

"Oh no," said Nathan. "I just keep coming back."

"And what does your mum think of that?"

"She doesn't mind," replied Nathan. "Is your bloat better?"

"Cleared itself," said Old McDonald mysteriously. "What do you get up to, all on your own in here?"

"I think," said Nathan.

"I was never much of a thinker at your age," said Old McDonald. "Or later," he added honestly.

"I've been working things out," continued Nathan. "About Peter Jonathan Hunter and the picture on the wall. Was he your friend, like Danny is mine?"

"He made out he was," said Old McDonald. "But when it come down to it, he had no one else."

"What was he like?"

"He was all fancy schemes and bright ideas and me to do the donkey work," said Old McDonald grumpily.

"Like in the picture? Him pointing and you digging?"

43

"That's right," said Old McDonald.

"The Miss Kents told me that in the war all the children were sent to the country. Did you have to go?"

"I was one of the first. My dad packed my mum and me off to my auntie's."

"What about Peter?"

"Whole family up and left a few weeks later. Left my dad to take care of things. Last I saw of any one of them. The house was sold for flats in the end."

"Did you never see Peter again?"

"It was no great loss if I didn't," said Old McDonald. "He wasn't to be trusted for all his promises."

"Was it in summer?"

"High summer," said Old McDonald. "All the roses were out."

Chapter Four

On Sunday morning, just after six o'clock, Chloe woke up.

"Morning at last!" said Nathan (which was not at all his usual reaction to his sister's dawn-time shrieks). This morning was different, however, and before his mother had time to say, "Stay where you are!" he was out of bed and dressed. For the next two hours or so, at roughly ten-minute intervals, he asked whether it was now late enough to go upstairs and visit Danny.

"No," said his mother, fourteen times at ten-minute intervals, but shortly after the fourteenth time she fell asleep and Nathan's father, when asked the same question, merely groaned.

* * *

"Nathan!" exclaimed Danny's mother, pulling open her front door to discover who was hammering on it at that hour of the morning. "Whatever is the matter?"

"Nothing," said Nathan cheerfully. "I've just come to call for Danny, that's all."

"It's Sunday morning!" said Danny's mother, clutching her dressing gown around her. "It's only just gone eight o'clock! I was asleep!"

"We've been up for hours," said Nathan. "Good old Chloe got us up at six but Mum wouldn't let me out before now."

"Whatever is so urgent?"

"Something in the garden. Tell Danny, please!"

"Danny!" called his mother, but Danny had heard and had tumbled out of bed in great excitement.

"Have the badgers come already?" he asked, heading for the door in his pyjamas.

"Much better than badgers," said Nathan. "We'll need your spade."

"What's better than badgers?"

"Secret," said Nathan.

"Well," said Danny's mother in disgust. "I'm going back to bed! Don't you dare stir a step without getting properly dressed, Danny! Have you had any breakfast, Nathan?"

"Ages ago," said Nathan.

"You'd better have another. Toast. Cereal. Milk. Goodnight!"

"You don't want breakfast," Nathan urged his friend when she had gone. "Hurry up! You can eat later."

"I do want breakfast," contradicted Danny. "If you don't eat breakfast your brain melts down."

"Melts down?"

"It gets used up instead of food."

"What guff!" said Nathan rudely.

"S'what my gran says," said Danny, and Nathan was forced to sit, bursting with impatience, while Danny slowly consumed slice after slice of toast and honey.

"Can't you eat any faster?" he demanded.

"No," said Danny.

"Well, lend me your spade and I'll start without you."

"No," said Danny. "You're not digging with my spade without me being there."

"Are you in a bad temper?" asked Nathan.

"No, I'm not. I just really thought for a minute that the badgers had come. Are you going to tell me what your precious secret is?"

"Treasure," said Nathan.

"What treasure?"

"The treasure in the garden in the picture."

"What picture?" asked Danny, still brooding about his missing badgers.

"The one we found under the stairs. I think your brain has melted down already!"

"You've gone crackers," said Danny. "Pass the butter. There wasn't any treasure in the picture."

"There's something," said Nathan positively. "And it might be treasure. People have always said about treasure in Paradise House. You know they have!"

"It's just a story."

"It might not be. Old McDonald came and talked to me last night. It was just how we guessed. He was friends with Peter. He said Peter was all fancy schemes and bright ideas . . ."

"Like you," interrupted Danny.

"And Peter promised Old McDonald he'd do something for him, and Old McDonald thinks he didn't do it. But I think he did. They both went away, just after that picture was painted. Old McDonald first, then Peter, and Peter never came back because

his family moved house. But I think he left a message for Old McDonald before he went and the message is the picture and the picture says, 'Dig where I'm pointing!' Plain as plain. 'Very important!' And the date. But Old McDonald never dug."

"I'll get the spade," said Danny, suddenly convinced.

They dug and dug. Danny's badger holes were insignificant in comparison. After an

hour or so of hard work they had excavated enough ground to house a dozen badgers. They took it in turns, and the turns grew shorter and shorter as they grew more and more tired, but they did not give up.

"There's Anna watching!" remarked Danny, pausing for breath and catching sight of her waving from her bedroom window. He waved back, and a moment later she came running out to see what they were doing.

"We're digging for treasure," Nathan told her. "But don't tell anyone until we've found it, will you?"

"I won't," promised Anna. "Can I dig, too?"

"You'll get all muddy," Nathan warned.

"I don't mind," said Anna. "Can I start a new hole of my own?"

"No," said Nathan. "In case you find it."

"But I want to find it," protested Anna.

"You can't dig then," said Nathan firmly. "You can watch if you like, or dig where we tell you, but I tracked it down and it's

Danny's spade, so it's only fair that we should find it."

"All right," agreed Anna, seeing the logic of this. "I'll watch then." And for some time she watched critically while Nathan and Danny toiled in the mud.

"It's taking ages," she remarked eventually.

"I know," said Danny, passing the spade to Nathan and wiping his hot face with his muddy hands.

"Mind that worm!" said Anna suddenly. "Oh, Nathan!"

"What?" asked Nathan.

"You cut it in half!"

"It doesn't matter," he told her. "They grow into two worms if they're cut in half."

"It still must hurt," said Anna.

"Of course it doesn't," replied Nathan. "Does it, Danny?"

"They probably think it's worth it," replied Danny.

"I wouldn't," said Anna.

"Anna!" groaned Nathan. "Do stop going on!"

"Well, you won't let me help," said Anna.

"I would," said Danny.

"All right," said Nathan, sensing Danny was about to mutiny, and giving in at once. "Go on, Anna, you can dig where you like."

"You said it wasn't fair before."

"Only if you dug up the treasure."

"I don't believe there is any treasure," said Anna. "I only thought there was because you wouldn't let me dig. I'm going indoors!"

"Girls!" exclaimed Nathan and Danny.

All through the morning people came out to laugh at them. Nathan's parents, Danny's mother and, later, his gran, the two Miss Kents and Arun from down the road. Everyone made the same rude remarks:

"Struck gold yet? You'll be in Australia by teatime! What are you making, a kangaroo trap?"

Only Old McDonald did not think it was funny. He came out, inspected their trainers in disgust, and said, "Don't you dare set foot in the house in that state.

Plastered to your eyeballs! If I have to clean it up I'll . . . "

"Have our livers?" suggested Nathan.

"No need to talk nasty," said Old McDonald.

By dinnertime they were exhausted and filthy. There had been a moment of huge excitement when their spade had struck something large and solid, followed by great disappointment when they saw that it was the remains of a garden gnome.

"We might as well give up," said Danny despondently when this appeared, and Nathan did not disagree.

They scraped their boots on Old McDonald's scraper, and so much earth came off that Old McDonald fetched a shovel and made them carry it back to the garden.

"Waste not, want not," said Old McDonald. "That's good soil that is, black as black and full of worms."

"Badgers like worms," said Danny. "Worms are their favourite food."

"Badgers," said Old McDonald scornfully. "Badgers would be ruination in a rose garden!"

"It isn't a rose garden," pointed out Danny.

"More's the pity!" said Old McDonald.

"What happened to the roses that used to be there?" asked Nathan suddenly. "Did somebody dig them up?"

"What kind of a fool would dig up roses?" demanded Old McDonald. "They was there right through the war and after. They should have been dug up in the war and vegetables grown instead, but my dad would have none of that and the roses stayed where they was. They were here till they started letting out the flats to people with children. Boys happened to the roses. Boys and bikes and football and chasings about. They were flattened years ago."

"Not by us!" said Nathan indignantly.

"Before your time," admitted Old McDonald.

"I wish they were still there," said Nathan when he had gone.

"I'd rather have badgers," said Danny.

"If they were still there," continued Nathan, ignoring him, "it would be much easier. We would know exactly where to dig."

"How?"

"We'd just find the rose in the picture and dig there."

The same thought occurred to both of them at once, and they rushed under the stairs and seized the picture from the wall.

"It's just like playing battleships," said Nathan excitedly. "Five roses out and nine from the edge of the grass."

"If he counted them properly when he drew the picture," added Danny.

"I bet he did. Look how carefully he's drawn them. Much better than anything else."

"Well, they're gone now," said Danny sighing. "I give up! I bet the treasure's gone too, if it was ever there! Anyway, I've got to go. It's one o'clock. It's dinnertime."

"Who cares about dinnertime?" asked Nathan.

"I do," said Danny. "I'm starving and it's

chicken and pineapple pudding! I'll see you later."

Nathan nodded but did not reply. His head was full of dreams of treasure. Treasure and roses and Old McDonald and Peter who had painted a picture. At dinnertime he ate without noticing what was on his plate, refused ice cream, and escaped, as soon as possible, to his lair under the stairs.

"Nathan!"

There was a tap at the door and his father's worried face appeared.

"Hallo," said Nathan.

"You all right in there?"

"Fine."

"I brought your ice cream. You sure you're all right? Not still fed-up about Chloe?"

"No."

"Nothing on your mind I can help you with?"

"I wish . . . " said Nathan.

"What do you wish?"

"I wish there were still roses at Paradise House," said Nathan.

"Roses!" exclaimed his father, so startled that he stood suddenly upright and hit his head on Nathan's ceiling. "Roses!" He reached up to feel the bump and cracked his elbow on the wall. "Roses!" He doubled up in agony and dropped Nathan's ice cream on his foot. "Roses!" said Nathan's father crossly. "I'm out of here!"

"You'd better clean up that ice cream," said Nathan reprovingly, "or Old McDonald will have your liver!"

"He'll have to come and get it first!" muttered Nathan's father irritably, but nevertheless he went back to the flat to find a mop. By the time he returned, Nathan had vanished.

Chapter Five

Old McDonald's Sunday dinner was always the same and always delicious. Every week he hotted up for himself one large tin of baked beans and one large tinned steak pie. He was just putting them on the kitchen table when Nathan hammered on the basement door.

"'Op it!" shouted Old McDonald, without even looking to see who it was.

Nathan banged again.

"I'm not coming!" shouted Old McDonald. "'Op it I say!"

"It's me!" called Nathan.

"I don't care if it's Father Flopping Christmas!" shouted back Old McDonald. "'Op it or I'll have your liver!"

"You'll have to come and get it first," said Nathan.

Old McDonald stamped across the kitchen and flung open the door. "You've had fair warning!" he announced threateningly. "And now I . . . Oh, it's you then, is it?" he finished in quite a different voice.

"Yes," said Nathan, "I . . . "

"Had your dinner?"

"Yes, I . . . "

"Like another?" asked Old McDonald, and before Nathan could reply he'd closed the door behind him, given him a chair, chopped the pie in half and divided it between two plates. He poured half a can of baked beans on to each piece of pie and handed one enormous plateful over to Nathan, before sitting down to the other himself.

"I . . . " began Nathan again.

"You eat that," said Old McDonald. "Calm you down! You're all aeriated!"

"But . . . "

"Your mum been trying to cook again?" asked Old McDonald.

Nathan nodded speechlessly, his mouth full of boiling hot baked beans.

"She wants to get in a few tins and put some flesh on you," said Old McDonald. "What about that pie, then? What do you think?"

"Lovely!" said Nathan as soon as he could speak.

"Smell it cooking, did you?" asked Old McDonald sympathetically.

"Oh no!" said Nathan hastily. "I came to ask you something. About roses."

"I believe in tins," said Old McDonald. "And for why? I'll tell you. They're made by experts!"

"I need an expert," said Nathan. "A rose expert."

"My dad was a rare chap for roses," said Old McDonald. "Now take your mum. She's not daft but she'll never cook anything equal to what comes out of a tin. And why's that? Because she's an amateur! Be a kindness to tell her but I don't suppose she'd thank you."

Nathan did not suppose she would either, but he refused to allow himself to be side-tracked.

"Did your dad plant the roses that used to

grow round Paradise House?" he asked.

"Every one of them," said Old McDonald. "He was an expert, if ever there was. He grew them by the book."

"What book?" asked Nathan.

"That there book on the cupboard over by the clock," said Old McDonald. "Sit down! Use a spoon to get your gravy up!"

Nathan, who had jumped to his feet, obediently sat down again and began to spoon up gravy. The huge helping of dinner (on top of the excellent meal already provided by his mother) had had a calming effect on him. He scraped his plate quite meekly while he asked, "Did he use that book to find out how far apart to plant them?"

"He didn't need telling that," said Old McDonald. "Three feet! Every fool knows that! Do you like treacle pudding?"

"Very much!" said Nathan, who, having eaten two dinners and discovered the key to buried treasure, felt equal to anything.

"Good," said Old McDonald. "I got one hotting up."

*　　*　　*

"Old McDonald," said Nathan over the pudding, "how long's three feet?"

"Distance between two roses," said Old McDonald with his mouth full.

"I mean how long does it look like?" asked Nathan.

"Don't they teach you nothing at school?"

"Centimetres," said Nathan.

"Them things is no use to no one," said Old McDonald scornfully. "See that?" He stuck out his foot. "That's one foot. Three is three of them."

"Are you sure?"

"Whose feet are they?" demanded Old McDonald. "Yours or mine?"

"Yours," said Nathan. "Old McDonald, will you listen if I talk to you for a bit?"

"What do you think I been doing all this time?" demanded Old McDonald.

For the rest of the meal Nathan explained his treasure-hunting theories to Old McDonald. He fetched the picture and showed him the clues and described how he and Danny had dug and dug all morning.

"I thought it was badgers you were after,"

interrupted Old McDonald at this point.

"Treasure," said Nathan. "But it was no good without knowing exactly where to dig. Danny gave up, but I thought and thought, and I thought if you know how many roses out and how many roses across and how far in between each rose, you could measure out exactly and find just where to dig."

"It's an idea," admitted Old McDonald.

"So now I need a measure that measures in feet. Have you got one I could borrow?"

"I got my feet," said Old McDonald.

"Come on, then!" said Nathan.

"Hold your horses," said Old McDonald. "Two things wrong."

"What?" demanded Nathan impatiently.

"One," said Old McDonald. "We haven't cleared up!"

Clearing up was easy. They threw the tins into the bin, ran their plates under the tap and left the knives and forks and spoons to soak.

"There!" said Nathan. "What's the other thing?"

"The other thing is Peter Hunter never

had no treasure," said Old McDonald. "He didn't have nothing. He never had tuppence to rub together."

"Treasure doesn't have to be money," interrupted Nathan.

"He had a few books and a handful of clothes, and that was about it," persisted Old McDonald. "All the time I knew him, that was all he had. They wasn't the sort of family that bought things for their kids. We lived in the basement but I had more than he did. He was forever borrowing stuff off of me. And he used to come down to our place when he wanted a bit of fun. That farm I had, he thought the world of it. He'd shift it around and make up tales . . . "

"The farm you lost?"

"I wouldn't say lost," said Old McDonald darkly.

"Five roses out from the wall and nine from the edge of the grass," said Nathan.

"You'll only be disappointed," said Old McDonald gloomily, but still he lumbered to his feet. Strange things were happening to Old McDonald. He couldn't remember the last time he had invited anyone into the basement flat, and he was sure he had never given anyone a meal in his life. Nobody since Peter Hunter had ever succeeded in talking him into anything. He wouldn't have believed that anyone in the world could force him into digging for treasure on a damp autumn afternoon, and, yet, here he was, following Nathan up the basement steps, carrying his father's best spade and feeling strangely young and excited.

"You made an 'orrible slobbing muck-heap out here," he observed, to cover up his feelings.

"Stand against the wall on the edge of the grass and measure fifteen feet," ordered Nathan, and when Old McDonald had solemnly paced out the distance, heel to toe, he made him turn to his left and pace out a further twenty-seven.

"Why twenty-seven?" asked Old McDonald.

"Three times nine roses," said Nathan. "Me and Danny were digging much too close to the wall this morning. No wonder we never found anything."

"You've made me lose count," grumbled Old McDonald. "I can't count and listen to you yattering at the same time. I ain't a computer."

"Start again!" ordered Nathan. "I'll count. You just walk."

"Listen to you!" exclaimed Old McDonald. "Laying down the law! You're Peter Hunter and it's me to do the donkey work all over again!"

"Now you've made *me* lose count!" said Nathan.

The third time they were lucky. They stood on the spot where, in the picture, the boy in the window pointed and the boy in the garden dug, and Old McDonald handed Nathan the spade.

"We'll take it in turns," said Nathan. "Five digs each."

"It was your daft idea," said Old McDonald.

"It's your treasure," said Nathan, and when he had finished his five digs he handed the spade back to Old McDonald.

"I never done such a darn silly thing in my life," grumbled Old McDonald, digging nevertheless. "If anyone were watching they'd laugh themselves sick. I don't know how I got talked into such airy-fairy nonsense. I . . . Hallo!"

Old McDonald's spade had hit something. They scraped at the earth and the remains of a sack appeared. It was quite rotten and fell to pieces in their hands as they tugged it. Inside the sack was a large, square bundle wrapped tightly in oilcloth. Inside

the bundle was a box, wooden and varnished, with letters on the lid.

"P.J.H.," read Nathan as Old McDonald, on his knees, gently lifted it from the ground.

"Well, I never," said Old McDonald. "Well, I'll be blowed! Well, I been a fool! Well, who'd . . . "

"Open it! Open it! Open it!" begged Nathan when it began to seem as if Old McDonald intended to spend the whole afternoon muttering on his knees in the mud.

"All these years it's been here!"

"*What*'s been here?" asked Nathan.

"All these years!" repeated Old McDonald. "And I could have had it out any time for five minutes' digging!"

"Had *what* out?" demanded Nathan.

"Now then!" said Old McDonald reprovingly. "No need to shout! I'd have thought you'd have guessed, and you so clever!"

"Guessed what?" pleaded Nathan.

Old McDonald's voice suddenly shook and dropped to a murmur.

"What's in this here box, of course!"
"What?" whispered Nathan.
"My old farm," said Old McDonald.

Chapter Six

"We'll take it inside to open it," said Old McDonald. "You'd better run and tell your mum where you'll be."

Nathan hovered in agony, unable to tear himself away from the box.

"Go on!" said Old McDonald. "'Op it!'"

"You won't open it until I come back?"

"What kind of a question is that?" asked Old McDonald scornfully.

"Sorry!" said Nathan and rushing up the steps into Paradise House, he shouted, "Mum! I'm down at Old McDonald's!" through the letter-box, and escaped before she could come out and ask questions. A moment later he was in Old McDonald's kitchen again.

"Right then!" said Old McDonald, and lifted the lid.

*　　*　　*

The box was full of little parcels, each care-fully wrapped in pieces of yellowed news-paper. On the top there was a letter.

"That'll be from 'im," said Old McDonald.

It was written in a scrawling, excited handwriting that sloped in all directions, as if the writer had been in a very great hurry. McDonald read it aloud while Nathan be-gan to unwrap the bundles.

"*Dear Old McDonald. We are leaving London in a rush hurray hurray at last it has been awful without you* . . ." Old McDonald paused and cleared his throat.

"*The house is to be packed up when we are gone and they say we might not come back* . . ."

"They didn't come back, did they?" asked Nathan. "I wonder what happened to Peter."

"He's still around," said Old McDonald. "Gets his name in the papers now and then. He's a nartist."

"What's a nartist?"

"Paints pictures," said Old McDonald. "What's that you got?"

Nathan held up a long line of ducks, each carefully enamelled in mallard colours.

"I remember him doing them," said Old McDonald. "He copied the colours off the ducks in the park."

"Did you paint them all yourselves?"

"Not all." Old McDonald searched through the collection of little metal animals already unwrapped. "Them horses with the harness on, he painted, and those three cockerels. Do you want to hear this letter or not?"

"Yes please."

"*I keep going down to the basement but your father is not there and you never sent your address like you said you would . . .*"

"You should have done if you said you would!" said Nathan severely. "Look! A tractor!"

"There should be a thresher somewhere," said Old McDonald. "I wasn't a great hand for writing.

". . . *So I am hiding the farm where no one could find it except you and leaving a picture in the stairhole to show you where to look.* Silly young idiot! Show me where to look! Why didn't he just leave the whole set-up under the stairs if my dad was away?"

"Because anyone might have taken it," said Nathan. "He wanted somewhere safe."

"So he says. *I know it will be all right in the rose-bed because I heard my father say to yours about digging it up to make room to grow food . . .*"

"Digging up the roses?" asked Nathan, shocked.

"*To grow food,*" continued Old McDonald. "*And your father said anyone lay a finger on my roses and I'll have his liver!*"

Nathan burst out laughing.

"What's the joke?" asked Old McDonald

sternly. "Break my dad's heart, it would, to see the garden the way it looks today."

"Well, you could plant some roses yourself," said Nathan.

"I've not got money to spend on roses. I'd have done it years ago if I had."

"Look!" said Nathan. "I've found the thresher. And a house and a barn and pigsties and piglets and pigs."

"Good," said Old McDonald.

"What else does Peter say?"

"He says, *I shouldn't mind the box back one day. It is the one Grandad made for me to take to school. P.J.H.*"

"You'll have to give it back to him, then," remarked Nathan, as he assembled a flock of sheep.

"How'm I supposed to do that?"

"I'll think of something," said Nathan cheerfully, and Old McDonald did not doubt that he would.

The little bundles of newspaper seemed endless. Nathan unwrapped one after another and gradually a whole farm appeared: cows and a bull with a ring through

its nose, sheep and lambs, chickens, ducks, geese, and a pigeon house with white pigeons on the roof, horses and foals, goats and pigs, sheep-dogs, sleeping cats, buildings and fences, and a whole family of farmers to take care of them all.

"There's even a windmill," said Nathan, unwrapping the last little parcel. "It's perfect! It's real treasure!"

"It's yours!" said Old McDonald.

"But he can't just keep it!" protested Nathan's mother, when she heard the news.

"Finders keepers," said Old McDonald. "He's welcome! Him and that Danny will enjoy it, and so will young Chloe one day."

"Things like that sell for an awful lot of money."

"T'aint for sale, though," said Old McDonald. "I'm not that short of a bob or two!"

"Nathan!" said Nathan's mother helplessly.

"I've given it to the boy," said Old McDonald stubbornly.

"Thank you," said Nathan.

"I don't think you should," argued Nathan's mother. "It doesn't seem right."

"'Course it's right," replied Old McDonald. "He'll need a new box to keep it in, though. I got that one promised to a friend." For, at Nathan's suggestion, Old McDonald had rung up every "Hunter, P.J." in the telephone book until he found the right one. Peter was coming to Paradise House that very night. It was to be a great occasion. Old McDonald already had a steak and kidney pudding hotting up and was happily opening tins of peaches, but Nathan's mother still worried.

"I didn't know what to do," she told his father that night. "He'll never take money, and we couldn't afford to give him what they're worth if he would."

"I know what he'd take," said Nathan.

"Pink!" said Nathan's mother. "Pink roses! My favourites! They have lovely bushes on the market, buy ten and get two free! I might go back for more!"

"It's the time of the year to plant roses," said Danny's gran, when the word got round. "I always fancy red myself. It's about time something was done with that garden!"

"Are we buying roses?" asked Anna's mother. "Fancy having a rose garden! I shall get yellow."

"And cream?" asked Anna. "And orange and gold?"

"I've never bought roses," said Danny's mother. "First time for everything! Do you think climbers would climb up the walls?"

"Of course they would," said the old Miss Kent. "And there's a rose called 'Peace'. Pink and yellow. I've ordered a dozen."

The young Miss Kent went suddenly pink and coy and ordered "Maiden's Blush".

"She needn't start getting ideas!" said Old McDonald to Nathan and Danny. "And who's to do the digging? And the pruning and the spraying? And they'll want bone meal and dried blood and slathers of muck!"

"Slathers of muck?" repeated Nathan with enjoyment.

"Me and Nathan have done most of the digging already," Danny pointed out. "And we've bought a rose. A blue one!"

"To plant where we found the treasure," said Nathan.

"Blue roses is vulgar!" said Old

McDonald. "And what's one blue rose going to look like in the middle of all them pinks and yellows?"

"It'll look beautiful," said Nathan.

"I don't know about beautiful," muttered Old McDonald, but he planted it anyway.

"They've got me going soft!" he grumbled to Peter one Sunday afternoon. "They've got me planting roses! They've about turned

my kitchen into a playhouse! They've got me cooking them dinners! They've even got me baby-sitting! Not that the baby's any trouble!"

"No trouble!" exclaimed Nathan, who was listening. "She screamed so much I had to go and live under the stairs!"

"Yes, and then what happened?" asked Peter. "If it hadn't been for Chloe, you'd never have found your treasure, and I'd never have got my box back, and Old

McDonald would still be living in peace!"

"Wasn't exactly peace," commented Old McDonald. "Don't know if it was exactly what I'd have called treasure, either!"

"It's *exactly* what *I*'d call treasure!" said Nathan.

"Perhaps you're right," said Old McDonald.

If you enjoyed reading *The Treasure in the Garden*, you might also like the other 'Paradise House' stories by Hilary McKay. Danny, Anna and Nathan continue their adventures in *The Zoo in the Attic* and, coming shortly, *The Echo in the Chimney* and *The Magic in the Mirror*.